# Bella and the Beautiful Fish

Written by Claire Llewellyn

Illustrated by Valeria Abatzoglu

**Collins**

# Who and what is in this story?

Listen and say

Download the audio at www.collins.co.uk/839718

🎧 Bella is at school. The teacher is telling them about the sea.

At home, Bella looks at books about the sea. She loves the pictures.

7

That night Bella goes to bed.

Bella closes her eyes. She sleeps and dreams.

Bella is on a beach. A beautiful red fish swims up to her. It wants her help.

Bella swims with the beautiful fish.
It takes her to a fishing net.

There you are!

The fish take Bella to their home in the sea.

15

After dinner, Bella and the fish swim back to the beach.

It is morning and Bella opens her eyes.

At school, Bella draws a picture of a ship under the sea.

What is the ship's name?

Bella's Dream.

# Picture dictionary

## Listen and repeat

beach

dream

fish

fishing net

sea

ship

swim

# 1 Look and order the story

# 2 Listen and say

# Collins

Published by Collins
An imprint of HarperCollins*Publishers*
Westerhill Road
Bishopbriggs
Glasgow
G64 2QT

HarperCollins*Publishers*
1st Floor, Watermarque Building
Ringsend Road
Dublin 4
Ireland

William Collins' dream of knowledge for all began with the publication of his first book in 1819.

A self-educated mill worker, he not only enriched millions of lives, but also founded a flourishing publishing house. Today, staying true to this spirit, Collins books are packed with inspiration, innovation and practical expertise. They place you at the centre of a world of possibility and give you exactly what you need to explore it.

© HarperCollins*Publishers* Limited 2020

10 9 8 7 6 5 4 3 2

ISBN 978-0-00-839718-0

Collins® and COBUILD® are registered trademarks of HarperCollins*Publishers* Limited

www.collins.co.uk/elt

British Library Cataloguing in Publication Data

A catalogue record for this publication is available from the British Library.

Author: Claire Llewellyn
Illustrator: Valeria Abatzoglu (Beehive)
Series editor: Rebecca Adlard
Commissioning editor: Zoë Clarke
Publishing manager: Lisa Todd
Product managers: Jennifer Hall and Caroline Green
In-house editor: Alma Puts Keren
Project manager: Emily Hooton
Editor: Tessie Papadopoulou-Dalton
Proofreaders: Natalie Murray and Michael Lamb
Cover designer: Kevin Robbins
Typesetter: 2Hoots Publishing Services Ltd
Audio produced by id audio, London
Reading guide author: Emma Wilkinson
Production controller: Rachel Weaver
Printed and bound by: GPS Group, Slovenia

MIX
Paper from
responsible sources
FSC www.fsc.org
FSC™ C007454

This book is produced from independently certified FSC™ paper to ensure responsible forest management.

For more information visit: **www.harpercollins.co.uk/green**

Download the audio for this book and a reading guide for parents and teachers at www.collins.co.uk/839718